Library of Congress Cataloging-in-Publication Data

Pank, Rachel.
Sonia and Barnie and the noise in the night / Rachel Pank.
p.   cm.

Summary: A young girl and her scared cat go out to investigate
after hearing a big noise in the night.

[1. Night—Fiction.   2. Noise—Fiction.   3. Cats—Fiction.]   I. Title.
PZ7.P18935   So   1991
[E]—dc20

ISBN 0-590-44657-6

12   11   10   9   8   7   6   5   4   3   2   1   1   2   3   4   5   6/9

Printed in Hong Kong by Imago Services (H.K.) Ltd.

First Scholastic printing, April 1991

Sonia and Barnie and the Noise in the Night

Rachel Pank

SCHOLASTIC
HARDCOVER

SCHOLASTIC INC. • NEW YORK

Sonia sat up. What was that? A strange
noise had awakened her. A noise that made
her arms get goose pimples and her hair stand up
(although she knew her hair usually stuck up a bit, anyway).

"Maybe it was baby Sam," she said to herself and went to look.

But baby Sam was wriggling and talking softly (well, his sort of talking) to his ducks.

"Coo, Sam," she said and tucked him up again.

"Maybe it was Barnie," she said to herself and went to look.

There was Barnie. His hair wasn't standing up but his ears were. Barnie had heard it, too.

They both went to look out of Sonia's
window into the dark garden.

At first Sonia could only see black,
but then she saw the bushes and then
the plants and, finally, she saw — it.

It was lit by the moon and had a
pointy nose like a dog, except it wasn't
a dog. And it was making that noise
again.

Sonia and Barnie looked at each
other and then they jumped into bed.

Sonia and Barnie and Teddy Bear
lay close together. Barnie wasn't
ordinarily allowed in bed,
but Sonia decided that
this was not an
ordinary night.

After a while they all fell
asleep, although every now and then a
strange noise came into their dreams. Sonia
woke early and couldn't wait for "wake-up time."

At breakfast, Sonia tried to tell Mom and Dad and baby Sam what she had seen. But they were more interested in playing with the free gift from the cereal box.

Sonia decided to announce the important news standing on her chair.

Barnie stood up, too.

But Mom just said, "Brush your hair, Sonia. It's standing straight up."

Sonia was very disappointed. She forgot to brush her hair and sat on the back step. Barnie sat very close, in a comforting sort of way.

Sonia thought. And thought. And suddenly she knew what it was. She knelt down in front of Barnie and spoke very slowly (like her teachers did when someone had been sick or a pair of scissors was missing).

"Look, Barnes, dear friend," Sonia began. Barnie blinked encouragingly. "Look Barnes, I know... I know what it is," her voice shook a bit. "It's a wolf."

Barnie got scared, and his tail bristled.

"Oh, Barnie," Sonia said, sounding a bit like Mom. "You look silly doing that when you don't have much fur."

Barnie slunk off into the bushes.

Sonia sighed. She'd have to get some of his Crunchie Wunchie cat biscuits now, or he'd sulk all day. To cheer herself up, she took a couple of people biscuits for herself.

They sat in the garden munching and watching ladybugs and bees and butterflies and ants going about their busy business.

This was one of their favorite sort of days. Not a very busy sort of day. But Sonia started to get restless. She wanted nighttime to come, to see if the wolf would return.

That night Sonia pretended to be asleep but, really, she was wide awake and playing hide-and-seek with Barnie. Barnie kept hiding,

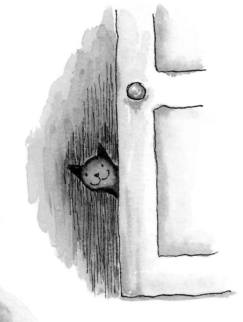

and then she would find him with her flashlight.

Suddenly – the noise!

A strange and spooky, howling, lonely sound. Barnie's
tail started to bristle again, but Sonia was impatient.
"Come on, Barnie!" she encouraged him. She
struggled into her bathrobe

and tiptoed

downstairs

as quickly

as she

could.

Standing in the garden with her bathrobe on backwards and Barnie all fluffed up and pretending to be brave (but standing behind her, she noticed), Sonia saw the wolf.

He held his sharp, pointy nose up to the moon and made the spooky noise again.

Barnie whimpered and tried to hide his ears but Sonia was in a fearless mood.

However, her knees did wobble a bit and her neck got ticklish as the wolf turned to face her. Sonia's mouth felt dry (like it did when she ate too many chips), and she could hear her heart beating loudly in her ears. She looked around for Barnie but he was up a tree.

Suddenly, Sonia giggled. She crouched in front of the wolf.

"Look, the thing is," she said slowly, like the teachers did, "the thing is... you're not really a wolf!

"You see," she went on patiently, "you've got the wrong tail!" And he did. It was long and very, very bushy. The wolf looked at it mournfully.

Barnie came down to look at such a thick tail. Sonia continued excitedly.

a fox!

a fox!

"I think, I think that what you are is a FOX!" The wolf pricked up his long reddish ears. "Yes," Sonia said, "a fox," and she spelt it slowly, like the teachers did, "F-O-X."

The wolf-who-was-really-a-fox turned around and
around as though he'd never seen himself before. He
looked at his tail and his paws and then sat down and put
his pointy nose up to the moon.

Sonia quickly put her hands over his mouth (which was
a little tricky, with a wolf-who-was-really-a-fox). "Oh, no,
you don't," she said firmly. "That's what wolves do, and
you are a fox." The fox gulped and Barnie took his paws
out of his ears.

Barnie was the first to hear the bushes
rustling. They all turned around to
see another fox (who-knew-it-was-
really-a-fox) standing there.

The wolf-who-was-really-a-fox went up to his new reddish friend. They sniffed each other (like animals do), and then they were off, scampering along the wall.

"Good-bye, dear friends," called Sonia, and the foxes waved their big, bushy tails.

Barnie walked in and out of Sonia's legs quickly, flicking his tail. He did not want her to forget that he was her "dear friend" firstly and most importantly. "I know, Barnes," Sonia said, picking him up. "I know."

Suddenly, her feet felt cold and so did her back (because her bathrobe was still on backwards).

She and Barnie went inside and they both had some biscuits (to warm up their feet). Then she got into bed with Teddy Bear, and Barnie snuggled on top (not ordinarily allowed), but of course this was not an ordinary night, Sonia thought.

They all dreamt about the two foxes playing in the moonlight.

At breakfast, Barnie washed
his face and yawned a lot.

Baby Sam was pointing at the cereal box and spitting
out bits of food.

"You know you shouldn't talk with your mouth full,
Sam," Sonia said absentmindedly (with a mouth
full of toast).

She started to pour herself some
cereal, when "plink!" the free gift
tumbled into her bowl.

A tiny plastic fox!

Sonia and Barnie never saw the wolf-who-was-really-a-fox again. But sometimes, on a bright, moonlit night, he crept softly into the garden to make a faint and friendly howl, which Sonia and Barnie heard in their dreams.